Stopping for Death

Stopping for Death

Edited by Carol Ann Duffy
Illustrated by Trisha Rafferty

VIKING

In memory of
Penny Tackaberry, 1946–1994

VIKING

Published by the Penguin Group
Penguin Books Ltd, 27 Wrights Lane, London W8 5TZ, England
Penguin Books USA Inc., 375 Hudson Street, New York, New York 10014,
USA
Penguin Books Australia Ltd, Ringwood, Victoria, Australia
Penguin Books Canada Ltd, 10 Alcorn Avenue, Toronto, Ontario,
Canada M4V 3B2
Penguin Books (NZ) Ltd, 182–190 Wairau Road, Auckland 10, New Zealand

Penguin Books Ltd, Registered Offices: Harmondsworth, Middlesex, England

First published 1996
1 3 5 7 9 10 8 6 4 2

This collection copyright © Carol Ann Duffy, 1996
Illustrations copyright © Trisha Rafferty, 1996

Printed in Great Britain by Clays Ltd, St Ives plc

A CIP catalogue record for this book is available from the British Library

ISBN 0–670–85416–6

Because I Could Not Stop for Death

Because I could not stop for Death –
He kindly stopped for me –
The Carriage held but just Ourselves –
And Immortality.

We slowly drove – He knew no haste
And I had put away
My labor and my leisure too,
For His Civility –

We passed the School, where Children strove,
At Recess – in the Ring –
We passed the Fields of Gazing Grain –
We passed the Setting Sun –

Or rather – He passed Us –
The Dews drew quivering and chill –
For only Gossamer, my Gown –
My Tippet – only Tulle –

We paused before a House that seemed
A Swelling of the Ground –
The Roof was scarcely visible –
The Cornice – in the Ground –

Since then – 'tis Centuries – and yet
Feels shorter than the Day
I first surmised the Horses' Heads
Were toward Eternity –

Emily Dickinson

Contents

Come From That Window Child

For Pat Rodney and her children, and the other thousands in whom Walter Rodney* lives on

Come from that window child
no use looking for daddy tonight
daddy not coming home tonight

Come from that window child
all you'll see is stars burning bright
you won't ever see daddy car light

Come from that window child
in your heart I know you asking why
in my heart too I wish the news was lie

Come from that window child
tonight I feel the darkness bleed
can't tell flower from seed

Come from that window child
to live for truth ain't no easy fight
when some believe power is their right

Come from that window child
a bomb blow up daddy car tonight
but daddy words still burning bright

Come from that window child
tonight you turn a man before your time
tonight you turn a man before your time

John Agard

*Walter Rodney, a Guyanese historian and revolutionary and author of *How Europe Underdeveloped Africa*, was killed on 13 October 1980 in Guyana.

Memento Mori

He died
we buried him
his first rain fell tonight

*Sabahattin Kudret Aksal,
trans. Feyyaz Kayacan Fergar*

3

Be Merry

Whenever you see the hearse go by
And think to yourself you're gonna die,
Be merry, my friends, be merry.

They put you in a big white shirt
And cover you over with tons of dirt,
Be merry, my friends, be merry.

They put you in a long-shaped box
And cover you over with tons of rocks,
Be merry, my friends, be merry.

The worms crawl out and the worms crawl in,
The ones that crawl in are lean and thin,
The ones that crawl out are fat and stout,
Be merry, my friends, be merry.

Your eyes fall in and your hair falls out
And your brains come tumbling down your snout,
Be merry, my friends, be merry.

Anon.

The Dying Airman

A handsome young airman lay dying,
And as on the aerodrome he lay,
To the mechanics who round him came sighing,
These last dying words did he say:

'Take the cylinders out of my kidneys,
The connecting-rod out of my brain,
Take the cam-shaft from out of my backbone,
And assemble the engine again.'

Anon.

The Unquiet Grave

'The wind doth blow to-day, my love,
  And a few small drops of rain;
I never had but one true love,
  In cold grave she was lain.

'I'll do as much for my true love
  As any young man may;
I'll sit and mourn all at her grave
  For a twelvemonth and a day.'

The twelvemonth and a day being up,
  The dead began to speak:
'Oh who sits weeping on my grave,
  And will not let me sleep?'

' 'Tis I, my love, sits on your grave,
  And will not let you sleep;
For I crave one kiss of your clay-cold lips,
  And that is all I seek.'

'You crave one kiss of my clay-cold lips;
  But my breath smells earthy strong;
If you have one kiss of my clay-cold lips,
  Your time will not be long.

' 'Tis down in yonder garden green,
    Love, where we used to walk,
The finest flower that ere was seen
    Is withered to a stalk.

'The stalk is withered dry, my love,
    So will our hearts decay;
So make yourself content, my love,
    Till God calls you away.'

Anon.

7

Poem

And if it snowed and snow covered the drive
he took a spade and tossed it to one side.
And always tucked his daughter up at night.
And slippered her the one time that she lied.

And every week he tipped up half his wage.
And what he didn't spend each week he saved.
And praised his wife for every meal she made.
And once, for laughing, punched her in the face.

And for his mum he hired a private nurse.
And every Sunday taxied her to church.
And he blubbed when she went from bad to worse.
And twice he lifted ten quid from her purse.

Here's how they rated him when they looked back:
sometimes he did this, sometimes he did that.

Simon Armitage

Funeral Blues

Stop all the clocks, cut off the telephone,
Prevent the dog from barking with a juicy bone,
Silence the pianos and with muffled drum
Bring out the coffin, let the mourners come.

Let aeroplanes circle moaning overhead
scribbling on the sky the message He Is Dead,
Put crêpe bows round the white necks of the public
    doves,
Let the traffic policemen wear black cotton gloves.

He was my North, my South, my East and West,
My working week and my Sunday rest,
My noon, my midnight, my talk, my song;
I thought that love would last forever: I was wrong.

The stars are not wanted now: put out every one;
Pack up the moon and dismantle the sun;
Pour away the ocean and sweep up the wood;
For nothing now can ever come to any good.

                                        W. H. Auden

Charlotte, Her Book

I am Charlotte. I don't say hello
to people and sometimes I bite.
Although I am dead I still jump
out of bed and wake them up at night.

This is my mother. Her hair is blue
and I have drawn her with no eyes
and arms like twigs. I don't do
what I'm told and I tell lies.

This is my father. He has a mouth
under his left ear. I'm fed up
with drawing people, so I scribble
smoke and cover his head right up.

I am a brat kid, fostered out because
my mother is sick in the head,
and I would eat her if I could,
and make her good and dead.

Although I am only four I went away
so soon they hardly knew me,
and stars sprang out of my eyes,
and cold winds blew me.

My mother always says she loves me.
My father says he loves me too.
I love Charlotte. A car ran
over Charlotte. This is her book.

Elizabeth Bartlett

Reincarnation

The wise old men
    of India say
There are certain rules.
For example, if you loved
your dog too much,
in your next life you'll be a dog,
yet full of human memories.
And if the King's favourite daughter
loved the low-caste palace gardener
who drowned while crossing the river
in a small boat during the great floods,
they'll be reborn, giving a second chance.
The wise old men of India say
one often dreams
of the life one led before.

There's a lion sprawled out
beside his cubs.
His thick mane tangled with dry grass,
his head droops: dusty stooping dahlia.
Then with a shudder,
    a sudden shake of his head
he groans and growls
at four whimpering cubs.
(He'd let them climb
all over his back
if only he weren't so hungry.)

The lioness is already far away
hunting in the deepest part of the valley:
a tall dark forest.
Red-flowered vines,
gold-flecked snakes encircling every tree.
Tall ferns,
fringes of maidenhair edging broad leaves.
But now the lioness steps out
into a vast clearing.
She lifts her head towards the east, the west:
sniffing, sniffing. Her eyes stare hard,
urgent, she walks as if her raw swollen teats,
pink and not quite dry, prickle and itch and goad
    her on.
She's lean enough, afraid
her cubs might die.
Now there's clear water flowing rapidly,
rippling over rocks, the lioness stops, drinks,
her quick long tongue licks, laps up the water.
Now the lioness is wading through, swimming,
her long golden tail streams through rushing waves;
torn, bruised paws splashing.
A quiet breeze
    as if the earth were barely breathing.
Fallen leaves, still green,
and tangled vines swirl in the water,
    the lioness circling.
Nearby monkeys, squirrels,
even birds remain hidden, silence.
A dead bull elephant rots:
    bullet-pocked, tuskless.

You hold me, rock me,
pull me out of my dream
(or did I dream you?).
The fur lingers on your skin,
your body has not forgotten
how to move like a cat.
Look, the sun spills golden over the walls,
you grow tawnier with the dawn.
Shivering haunches relax,
the slow licking begins
gently over the bruises.

Sujata Bhatt

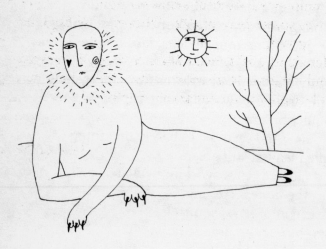

14

The Soldier

If I should die, think only this of me:
That there's some corner of a foreign field
That is for ever England. There shall be
In that rich earth a richer dust concealed;
A dust whom England bore, shaped, made aware,
Gave, once, her flowers to love, her ways to roam,
A body of England's, breathing English air,
Washed by the rivers, blest by suns of home.

And think, this heart, all evil shed away,
A pulse in the eternal mind, no less
Gives somewhere back the thoughts by England
    given;
Her sights and sounds; dreams happy as her day;
And laughter, learnt of friends; and gentleness,
In hearts at peace, under an English heaven.

Rupert Brooke

Kirkyard

A silent conquering army,
The island dead,
Column on column, each with a stone banner
Raised over his head.

A green wave full of fish
Drifted far
In wavering westering ebb-drawn shoals beyond
Sinker or star.

A labyrinth of celled
And waxen pain.
Yet I come to the honeycomb often, to sip the finished
Fragrance of men.

George Mackay Brown

To Edward Fitzgerald

I chanced upon a new book yesterday:
I opened it, and, where my finger lay
'Twixt page and uncut page, these words I read
– Some six or seven at most– and learned thereby
That you, Fitzgerald, whom by ear and eye
She never knew, 'thanked God my wife was dead.'
Ay, dead! and were yourself alive, good Fitz,
How to return you thanks would task my wits:
Kicking you seems the common lot of curs –
While more appropriate greeting lends you grace:
Surely to spit there glorifies your face –
Spitting from lips once sanctified by Hers.

Robert Browning

Cat's-eyes

The cat was killed
   the other day
crossing the line
   on the carriageway.

I liked her eyes.
   They moved between
a gold like honey
   and emerald green.

The pupils narrowed
   or went wide
from top to bottom
   and side to side.

I think at moments
   I have seen
a light behind
   the gold or green –

a sort of ember
  turning bright
in shadowy places
  or at night.

At dusk the carriageway
  will shine
with Cat's–eyes opening
  down the line.

Conor Carson

Who's That Up There?

'Who's that up there?'
Called Jinny-lie-by-the-Church.

'Didn't hear a sound
All morning,'
Said Tom Snoring.

'Nor I,'
Said Little Jack Found.

'Seeming you're dreaming,'
Grizzled old Grannie Mutton.

'Children at play!'
Yawned Ben-sleep-till-Doomsday.

'Certainly so,'
Breathed Danny Button.

Said Jinny, 'Well,
I fancy I hear a bell
And Parson Hook
Mumbling out of his book,
And feet that do tread
The green overhead.'

'Think you're right,'
Muffled Granfer Blight.

'I'm sure as sure
Someone or other,
Middle of summer,
Is coming to make
One more.'

'Ain't enough room,'
Whispered Sally Coombe.
'Best they held steady.
Bit of a squash here
Already.'

'Hope it ain't Fiddler Niall,
Him with the teeth and the smile,'
Said Long Tommy Tile.

'Or Journeyman Seth,
Hedger and ditcher,
Him with the cider
On his breath,'
Said Peter the Preacher.

'Or that Mrs Handle,
Talks nothing but scandal,
Or young Peter Blunder
With the bull-chest and the voice
Like thunder,'
Said Bessie Boyce.

'Or Jessie Priddle the teacher
– Bossy old creature –
She'd soon tell us all
What to do,'
Said Barty Blue.

'Oh dear!' they sighed
With a groan.

'Why can't they leave us
Alone?'
Cried Crusty-the-Baker.
'It's peaceful and easeful
We are
In God's little acre.'

Charles Causley

Yama*

Yama, when my hour comes,
I know you will be there:
solemn, dark and steadfast,
your buffalo pawing
the ground. You are waiting.
I will gladly follow.
I am certain of you,
at least, in this restless
world of humanity.
The sheet you'll wrap around
me is your cloak of peace.
You have gone through this mill
before me,
led so many brothers
and sisters after you,
so you will guide me too.
Yama, when my hour comes,
I know you'll not fail me.

But tell me,
Yama, when your time came,
who came to steer you to
the land that is now yours?
I will gladly follow
you, Guru, on that one
condition.

Debjani Chatterjee

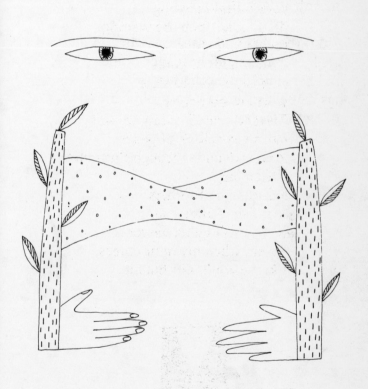

*In Hindu mythology Yama was the first man to die. He became the King of
the Underworld and God of Death.

the death of thelma sayles

2/13/59
age 44

i leave no tracks so my live loves
can't follow. at the river
most turn back, their souls shivering,
but my little girl stands alone on the bank
and watches. i pull my heart out of my pocket
and throw it. i smile as she catches all
she'll ever catch and heads for home
and her children. mothering
has made it strong, i whisper in her ear
along the leaves.

Lucille Clifton

imagining bear

for alonzo moore sr.

imagine him too tall and too wide
for the entrance into parlors

imagine his hide gruff, the hair on him
grizzled even to his own hand

imagine his odor surrounding him,
rank and bittersweet as bark

imagine him lumbering as he moves
imagine his growl filling the wind

give him an old guitar
give him a bottle of booze

imagine his children laughing; papa papa
imagine his wife sighing; oh lonnie

imagine him singing, imagine his granddaughter
remembering him in poems

Lucille Clifton

The Dead

The dead are always looking down on us, they say,
while we are putting on our shoes or making a
    sandwich,
they are looking down through the glass-bottom
    boats of heaven
as they row themselves slowly through eternity.

They watch the tops of our heads moving below on
    earth,
and when we lie down in a field or on a couch,
drugged perhaps by the hum of a warm afternoon,
they think we are looking back at them,

which makes them lift their oars and fall silent
and wait, like parents, for us to close our eyes.

Billy Collins

Endangered

It is so quiet on the shore of this motionless lake
you can hear the slow recessional of extinct animals
as they leave through a door at the back of the
    world,
disappearing like the verbs of a dead language:

the last troop of kangaroos hopping out of the
    picture,
the ultimate paddling of ducks and pitying of
    turtledoves
and, his bell tolling in the distance, the final goat.

Billy Collins

An Unusual Cat-Poem

My cat is dead.
But I have decided not to make a big
                                    tragedy out of it.

Wendy Cope

Tich Miller

Tich Miller wore glasses
with elastoplast-pink frames
and had one foot three sizes larger than the other.

When they picked teams for outdoor games
she and I were always the last two
left standing by the wire-mesh fence.

We avoided one another's eyes,
stooping, perhaps, to re-tie a shoelace,
or affecting interest in the flight

of some fortunate bird, and pretended
not to hear the urgent conference:
'Have Tubby!' 'No, no, have Tich!'

Usually they chose me, the lesser dud,
and she lolloped, unselected,
to the back of the other team.

At eleven we went to different schools.
In time I learned to get my own back,
sneering at hockey-players who couldn't spell.

Tich died when she was twelve.

Wendy Cope

My Grandmother's Love Letters

There are no stars tonight
But those of memory.
Yet how much room for memory there is
In the loose girdle of soft rain.

There is even room enough
For the letters of my mother's mother,
Elizabeth,
That have been pressed so long
Into a corner of the roof
That they are brown and soft,
and liable to melt as snow.

Over the greatness of such a space
Steps must be gentle.
It is all hung by an invisible white hair.
It trembles as birch limbs webbing the air.

And I ask myself:

'Are your fingers long enough to play
Old keys that are but echoes:
Is the silence strong enough
To carry back the music to its source
And back to you again
As though to her?'

Yet I would lead my grandmother by the hand
Through much of what she would not understand;
And so I stumble. And the rain continues on the roof
With such a sound of gently pitying laughter.

Hart Crane

Killed in Action

For N. J. de B.–L.
Crete, May, 1941

His chair at the table, empty,
His home clothes hanging in rows forlorn,
His cricket bat and cap, his riding cane,
The new flannel suit he had not worn.
His dogs, restless, with tortured ears
Listening for his swift, light tread upon the path.
And there – his violin! Oh his violin! Hush! hold
    your tears.

Juliette de Bairacli-Levy

We Do Not Play on Graves

We do not play on graves
Because there isn't room;
Besides, it isn't even,
It slants, and people come

And put a flower on it,
And hang their faces so,
We're fearing that their hearts will drop
And crush out pretty play.

And so we move as far
As enemies away,
Just looking round to see how far
It is, occasionally.

Emily Dickinson

Pathetic Magic

At the door
the love we want to offer
gathers itself.

Safe Home, Take Care,
Good Luck, God Bless,
a rabbit's foot.

Nothing saves us
from the boat tossed over,
a leaf in storm,

like my heart
turning now,
as darkness takes you,

and somewhere
a door slams,
long, long into the night.

Maura Dooley

Tullynoe: Tête-a-Tête in the Parish Priest's Parlour

'Ah, he was a grand man.'
'He was: he fell out of the train going to Sligo.'
'He did: he thought he was going to the lavatory.'
'He did: in fact he stepped out of the rear door of the train.'
'He did: God, he must have got an awful fright.'
'He did: he saw that it wasn't the lavatory at all.'
'He did: he saw that it was the railway tracks going away from him.'
'He did: I wonder if... but he was a grand man.'
'He was: he had the most expensive Toyota you can buy.'
'He had: well, it was only beautiful.'
'It was: he used to have an Audi.'
'He had: as a matter of fact he used to have two Audis.'
'He had: and then he had an Avenger.'
'He had: and then he had a Volvo.'
'He had: in the beginning he had a lot of Volkses.'
'He had: he was a great man for the Volkses.'
'He was: did he once have an Escort?'
'He had not: he had a son a doctor.'
'He had: and he had a Morris Minor too.'
'He had: he had a sister a hairdresser in Kilmallock.'
'He had: he had another sister a hairdresser in Ballybunion.'

'He had: he was put in a coffin which was put in his father's cart.'
'He was: his lady wife sat on top of the coffin driving the donkey.'
'She did: ah, but he was a grand man.'
'He was: he was a grand man...'
'Good night, Father.'
'Good night, Mary.'

Paul Durcan

The Baffling Dead

There is no vocabulary
for this, the no-language
of grief. I can reveal
what my brain thinks,
but where are words
for this vague pain I feel?

So the world says it for me,
in sudden glimpses
of old men everywhere,
stout in light raincoats
and flat caps,
with grey moustache and hair.

Behind me in a shop
I hear his sniff
or the timbre of his talk,
see someone else half-blind
swaying, hesitating
with his careful walk.

And memory says it for me
in unexpected snapshots,
seconds of total recall.
I am sixteen.
He hunches out of the front
door as I stand in the hall.

39

Suddenly I am swaying
to school in a small seat
on his bike. I write
him a poem quickly
in bed before he comes
to say goodnight.

I lie in bed
and hear him laughing and arguing
in the room below.
I show him my report.
'Why not all A's?'
he wants to know.

He opens a can of beer or,
established in an armchair
like a rounded hill,
pours scorn at the News,
settled in his comforts,
searing in his views.

And all I can think is
'This was my father
and he is not here now.'
No words for the strangeness of death
and the complex unwilled collage
the baffling dead endow.

Irene Earis

The Old Deaths

In the Twenties, when I was ten or more,
my mother used to tell me about the deaths of old
    people –
perhaps this was to forestall questions like:
'Why don't we go to see Aunt Annie any more?'

She would say, 'You remember old Mrs Something?
Well, she's died.' There were never any details –
as now, being grown-up, we might easily say
'It was cancer of the larynx,' or something of the
    something.

I never asked. I wasn't very curious.
Dying, like smoking, was a thing that grown-ups
    did.
Let them get on with it, would be roughly my
    attitude.
I accepted it as part of life; it wasn't odd or curious.

Aunt Annie lived close, among Eastern souvenirs –
she had quite a big ivory temple or pagoda,
kept under glass. She was nice, and gave me
    chocolates.
She was small, like Queen Victoria. Such thoughts
    are souvenirs,

they are talismans and tokens; not emotional
  rememberings.
These were the lives I scarcely touched, I brushed
  against them.
Perhaps I was aware of an atmosphere of kindness –
an old arthritic lady, in a chair, among
  rememberings.

NOTE She was my mother's aunt, my great-aunt.

Gavin Ewart

42

The Suicides

It is hard for us to enter
the kind of despair they must have known
and because it is hard we must get in by breaking
the lock if necessary for we have not the key,
though for them there was no lock and the
   surrounding walls
were supple, receiving as waves, and they drowned
though not lovingly; it is we only
who must enter in this way.

Temptations will beset us, once we are in.
We may want to catalogue what they have stolen.
We may feel suspicion; we may even criticize the
   decor
of their suicidal despair, may perhaps feel
it was incongruously comfortable.

Knowing the temptations then
let us go in
deep to their despair and their skin and know
they died because words they had spoken
returned always homeless to them.

Janet Frame

Dirge for Unwin

Uncle Unwin
lived unwed,
died unmourned,
our tears unshed,
his chin unshaved,
his soul unsaved,
his feet unwashed,
his cat unfed,

uncouth, unkempt,
no cuff unfrayed,
his floor unswept,
his bed unmade,
ungenerous,
unkind to us,
the undertaker's
bill unpaid

until
his will,
found undercover,
left untold wealth
to an unknown lover.
It's so unfair.
We were unaware:
even nobodies count
on one another.

Philip Gross

Cynic's Epitaph

A race with the sun as he downed
I ran at evetide,
Intent who should first gain the ground
And there hide.

He beat me by some minutes then,
But I triumphed anon,
For when he'd to rise up again
I stayed on.

Thomas Hardy

Epitaph on a Pessimist

I'm Smith of Stoke, aged sixty-odd,
I've lived without a dame
From youth-time on; and would to God
My Dad had done the same.

Thomas Hardy

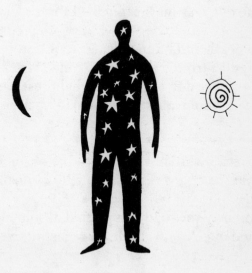

A Dog Was Crying Tonight in Wicklow Also

In memory of Donatus Nwoga

When human beings found out about death
They sent the dog to Chukwu with a message:
They wanted to be let back to the house of life.
They didn't want to end up lost forever
Like burnt wood disappearing into smoke
And ashes that get blown away to nothing.
Instead, they saw their souls in a flock at twilight
Cawing and headed back for the same old roosts
And the same bright airs and wing-stretchings each
    morning.
Death would be like a night spent in the wood:
At first light they'd be back in the house of life
(The dog was meant to tell all this to Chukwu).

But death and human beings took second place
When he trotted off the path and started barking
At another dog in broad daylight just barking
Back at him from the far bank of a river.

And that was how the toad reached Chukwu first,
The toad who'd overheard in the beginning
What the dog was meant to tell. 'Human beings,'
    he said,
(And here the toad was trusted absolutely),
'Human beings want death to last forever.'

48

Then Chukwu saw the people's souls in birds
Coming towards him like black spots off the sunset
To a place where there would be neither roosts nor
    trees
Nor any way back to the house of life.
And his mind reddened and darkened all at once
And nothing that the dog would tell him later
Could change that vision. Great chiefs and great
    loves
In obliterated light, the toad in mud,
The dog crying out all night behind the corpse
    house.

Seamus Heaney

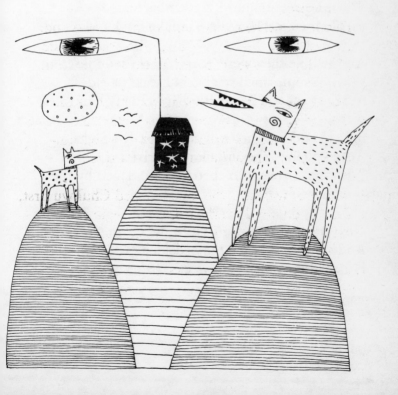

Mid-term Break

I sat all morning in the college sick bay
Counting bells knelling classes to a close.
At two o'clock our neighbours drove me home.

In the porch I met my father crying –
He had always taken funerals in his stride –
And Big Jim Evans saying it was a hard blow.

The baby cooed and laughed and rocked the pram
When I came in, and I was embarrassed
By old men standing up to shake my hand

And tell me they were 'sorry for my trouble'.
Whispers informed strangers I was the eldest,
Away at school, as my mother held my hand

In hers and coughed out angry tearless sighs.
At ten o'clock the ambulance arrived
With the corpse, stanched and bandaged by the
    nurses.

Next morning I went up into the room. Snowdrops
And candles soothed the bedside; I saw him
For the first time in six weeks. Paler now,

Wearing a poppy bruise on his left temple,
He lay in the four-foot box as in his cot.
No gaudy scars, the bumper knocked him clear.

A four-foot box, a foot for every year.

Seamus Heaney

51

Local Story

Old, often avoided,
she took it on herself
to scatter seed for the birds
about the churchyard

and the dead man joined in:
three tall sunflowers
from his belly rose

Libby Houston

Loss

A tulip fell deid
bi ma doorstep the day
dark rid the colour o' blood.
Wis the only yin come up this year.
A imagine it fell wi' a thud.

Alan Jackson

Every Dying Man

is a child:
in trenches, in bed, on a throne, at a loom,
we are tiny and helpless
when black velvet bows our eyes
and the letters slide from the pages.
Earth lets nobody loose: it all
has to be given back – breath, eyes, memory.
We are children when the earth
turns with us through the night toward morning
where there are no voices, no ears, no light, no door,
only darkness and movement
in the soil and its thousands
of mouths, chins, jaws, and limbs
dividing everything so that
no names and no thoughts remain
in the one who is silent lying in the dark
on his right side, head upon knees.
Beside him, his spear, his knife
and his bracelet, and a broken pot.

Jaan Kaplinski

Brendon Gallacher

He was seven and I was six, my Brendon Gallacher.
He was Irish and I was Scottish, my Brendon
   Gallacher.
His father was in prison; he was a cat burglar.
My father was a communist party full-time worker.
He had six brothers and I had one, my Brendon
   Gallacher.

He would hold my hand and take me by the river
Where we'd talk all about his family being poor.
He'd get his mum out of Glasgow when he got
   older.
A wee holiday some place nice. Some place far.
I'd tell my mum about my Brendon Gallacher.

How his mum drank and his daddy was a cat
   burglar.
And she'd say, 'Why not have him round to dinner?'
No, no, I'd say, he's got big holes in his trousers.
I like meeting him by the burn in the open air.
Then one day after we'd been friends two years

One day when it was pouring and I was indoors,
My mum says to me, 'I was talking to Mrs Moir
Who lives next door to your Brendon Gallacher
Didn't you say his address was 24 Novar?
She says there are no Gallachers at 24 Novar.

There never had been any Gallachers next door.'
And he died then, my Brendon Gallacher,
Flat out on my bedroom floor, his spiky hair,
His impish grin, his funny flapping ear.
Oh Brendon. Oh my Brendon Gallacher.

Jackie Kay

The Stincher

When I was three, I told a lie.
To this day that lie is a worry.

Some lies are too big to swallow;
some lies so gigantic they grow

in the dark ballooning and blossoming;
some lies tell lies and flower,

hyacinths; some develop extra tongues,
purple and thick. This lie went wrong.

I told my parents my brother drowned.
I watched my mother chase my brother's name,

saw her comb the banks with her fingers
down by the river Stincher.

I chucked a stone into the deep brown water,
drowned it in laughter; my father puffing,

found my brother's fishing reel and stool
down by the river Stincher.

I believed in the word disaster.
Lies make things happen, swell, seed, swarm.

Years from that away-from-home lie,
I don't know why I made my brother die.

I shrug my shoulders, when asked, raise my
eyebrows: *I don't know, right, I was three.*

Now I'm thirty-three. That day they rushed me
to the family friends' where my brother sat

undrowned, not frothing at the mouth, sat
innocent, quiet, watching the colourful TV.

Outside, the big mouth of the river Stincher
pursed its lips, sulked and ran away.

Jackie Kay

58

Grandfather

For me
He was the unassailable giant.
The creator of bicycles and dolls,
The law of God behind his butcher's apron.

He smelt
Of sausages and fresh air,
And he grew out of his small town
As naturally as a Black Forest pine tree.

Not quite
In tune he would sing to me,
With tears in his voice and eyes,
His well-worn folk-songs and ballads.

His word
Was gospel to his family,
And his wife's large domesticity
Was ornament and shape for his great size.

No one
Dared to correct him.
For him it was right to stub his roll,
To saturate his moustache and napkin,

So when
One April Fool's Day
They barricaded his shop and house,
He, like an angry god, turned away
from the living.

Lotte Kramer

Post Mortem

I met her in the market on the day
Her dog had died. And she, so shy and sparse
Of speech at other times, spilled grief among

The cabbages. 'He must have had a heart
Condition and we never realized,
We smacked and scolded him for muddy paws

When he came in, and then he just collapsed!
We blame ourselves, we should have coddled him.'
And so she fluttered on in her distress:

'There'll be an autopsy, we have to know.'
Then she begged pardon for her riot words
And hid behind the burden of her eyes.

Lotte Kramer

Lady in Black

Lady in black,
I knew your son.
Death was our enemy
Death and his gun.

Death had a trench
And he blazed away.
We took that trench
By the end of the day.

Lady in black
Your son was shot.
He was my mate
And he got it hot.

Death's a bastard
Keeps hitting back.
But a war's a war
Lady in black

Birth hurt bad
But you didn't mind.
Well maybe Death
Can be just as kind.

So take it quiet
The same as your son.
Death's only a vicar
Armed with a gun.

And one day Death
Will give it back
And then you can speak to him tidy
Lady in black.

Alun Lewis

Sorting Through

The moment she died, my mother's dancedresses
turned from the colours they really were
to the colours I imagine them to be. I can feel
the weight of bumptoed silver shoes
swinging from their anklestraps as she swaggers
up the path towards her Dad, light-headed
from airman's kisses. Every duster prints her
even more vivid than an Ilford snapshot on some
    seafront
in a white cardigan and that exact frock.
Old lipsticks. Liquid stockings.
Labels like Harella, Gor-ray, Berketex.
And, as I manhandle whole outfits into binbags for
    Oxfam,
every mote in my eye is a utility mark
and this is useful:
the sadness of dispossessed dresses,
the decency of good coats roundshouldered
in the darkness of wardrobes,
the gravitas of labels,
the invisible danders of skin fizzing off from them
like all that life that will not neatly end.

Liz Lochhead

Detour

I want my funeral to include this detour
Down the single street of a small market town,
On either side of the procession such names
As Philbin, O'Malley, MacNamara, Keane.
A reverent pause to let a herd of milkers pass
Will bring me face to face with grubby parsnips,
Cauliflowers that glitter after a sunshower,
Then hay rakes, broom handles, gas cylinders.
Reflected in the slow sequence of shop windows
I shall be part of the action when his wife
Calls to the butcher to get ready for dinner
And the publican descends to change a barrel.
From behind the one locked door for miles around
I shall prolong a detailed conversation
With the man in the concrete telephone kiosk
About where my funeral might be going next.

Michael Longley

Girlfriend

March 27, 1990

It's almost a year and I still
can't deal with you
not being
at the end of the line.

I read your name in memorial poems
and think they must be insane
mistaken malicious
in terrible error
just plain wrong

not that there haven't been times before
months passing madly sadly
we not speaking
get off my case, will you please?
oh, just lighten up!

But I can't get you out
of my air my spirit
my special hotline phone book
is this what it means to live
forever when will I
not miss picking up the receiver
after a pregnancy of silence
one of us born again
with a brand-new address or poem
miffed
because the other doesn't jump
at the sound
of her beloved voice?

Audre Lorde

The Lesson

'Your father's gone,' my bald headmaster said.
His shiny dome and brown tobacco jar
Splintered at once in tears. It wasn't grief.
I cried for knowledge which was bitterer
Than any grief. For there and then I knew
That grief has uses – that a father dead
Could bind the bully's fist a week or two;
And then I cried for shame, then for relief.

I was a month past ten when I learnt this:
I still remember how the noise was stilled
In school-assembly when my grief came in.
Some goldfish in a bowl quietly sculled
Around their shining prison on its shelf.
They were indifferent. All the other eyes
Were turned towards me. Somewhere in myself
Pride like a goldfish flashed a sudden fin.

Edward Lucie-Smith

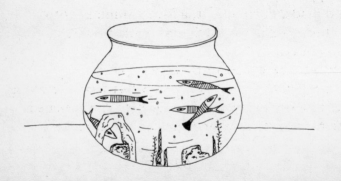

A Family of Fishermen

In all his dreams of death it was his heart that failed
    him.
It ran in the family like bellies and tempers
and though his mother's people favoured the long
    pull
and died mostly of kidneys or pneumonias,
skinny and bewildered in their nineties, all
the men drank whiskey and died of big hearts,
huffing and puffing to their purple ends.
So he held to his history and was ever ready
for one bolt out of nowhere that would lay him low
with only the juice left for one last wisdom,
maybe: *I always loved you* or *I told you so*
or *I must be dreaming*. He must have dreamt
a hundred times of how his great-great-grandfather
after a half day's fishing the cliffs at Doonlickey
could feed the whole parish on pollack and mackerel
till one day somehow he turned up missing
and washed up later in the bay at Goleen
wrapped up in his tackle of ribbons and sinkers
and made, in spite of it, a lovely summer corpse.
So he lit out in the pitch dark with the same
    instincts,
crossing the winter of his lake to where
he banged at the bare ice till his heart was breaking,
because of beauty, because the cold stars seemed
the blank eyes of women he had always loved,

and he told them so and thought he must be
   dreaming
to see his family, a family of fishermen,
approaching as the day broke under snowfall, so
he lay down in the first few inches of it.

Thomas Lynch

In Paradisum

Sometimes I look into the eyes of corpses.
They are like mirrors broken, frozen pools,
or empty tabernacles, doors left open,
vacant and agape; like votives cooling,
motionless as stone in their cold focus.
As if they'd seen something. As if it all
came clear to them, at long last, in that last moment
of light perpetual or else the black
abyss of requiems and nothingness.
Only the dead know what the vision is,
beholding which they wholly faint away
amid their plenary indulgences.
In Paradisum, deducante we pray:
their first sight of what is or what isn't.

                                        Thomas Lynch

The Patients

There are five patients I have to tell you about.
Michael first, with his nid-nodding head
And his love of Christian names, Jason from Bedford
Who has twenty seconds' warning
Before his attacks – time to stop the car –
And Roger who never smiles.

I mean, if you were Roger, penned in a chair
At the age of thirty-two, I wonder
If you would smile? Peter thinks not,
Painting the agile young Indian from Brixton
With his left hand, the only part
Not affected by his disease.

'Do you still have erections?' they ask,
That 'still' hovering like the blade
Of the guillotine. Doctors are mean,
Mustapha thinks, whom they ask often
While they toy with the pit of his arm.
An operation perhaps

Will carry Mustapha past forty. There remains
Colder comfort for the others. At home now
Soldiering on with my limp and my cough
I remember Michael and Jason, Roger and Peter
And Mustapha,

Those foot soldiers in the long retreat
From the Moscow of getting well
And I say a prayer:

Dear God, who created the human condition
And put the pain and death in the bottle,
Let there be Scotch and water for those poor sinners
Who have no more hope, and a shot of morphine
To carry them through.

George Macbeth

Memorial

Everywhere she dies. Everywhere I go she dies.
No sunrise, no city square, no lurking beautiful
   mountain
but has her death in it.
The silence of her dying sounds through
the carousel of language, it's a web
on which laughter stitches itself. How can my hand
clasp another's when between them
is that thick death, that intolerable distance?

She grieves for my grief. Dying, she tells me
that bird dives from the sun, that fish
leaps into it. No crocus is carved more gently
than the way her dying
shapes my mind. But I hear, too,
the other words,
black words that make the sound
of soundlessness, that name the nowhere
she is continuously going into.

Ever since she died
she can't stop dying. She makes me
her elegy. I am a walking masterpiece,
a true fiction
of the ugliness of death.
I am her sad music.

Norman MacCaig

Interruption to a Journey

The hare we had run over
Bounced about the road
On the springing curve
Of its spine.

Cornfields breathed in the darkness.
We were going through the darkness and
The breathing cornfields from one
Important place to another.

We broke the hare's neck
And made that place, for a moment,
The most important place there was,
Where a bowstring was cut
And a bow broken for ever
That had shot itself through so many
Darknesses and cornfields.

It was left in that landscape.
It left us in another.

Norman MacCaig

John Standish is Dead

In solemn tones
the head announced
'John Standish is dead'

It was a kind of
glamorous vanishing

an empty desk
assembly stretching into
double Maths (h'ray!)

& somehow it made me
fancy his sister Pauline

I so wanted to touch
her bright moon face
the magic of grief

Alan McDonald

Let Me Die a Youngman's Death

Let me die a youngman's death
not a clean & inbetween
the sheets holywater death
not a famous-last-words
peaceful out of breath death

When I'm 73
& in constant good tumour
may I be mown down at dawn
by a bright red sports car
on my way home
from an allnight party

Or when I'm 91
with silver hair
& sitting in a barber's chair
may rival gangsters
with hamfisted tommyguns burst in
& give me a short back & insides

Or when I'm 104
& banned from the Cavern
may my mistress
catching me in bed with her daughter
& fearing for her son
cut me up into little pieces
& throw away every piece but one

Let me die a youngman's death
not a free from sin tiptoe in
candle wax and waning death
not a curtain's drawn by angels borne
'what a nice way to go' death.

Roger McGough

Soles

'I caught four soles this morning,'
said the man with the beard;
cloud shifted and a sun-shaft pierced the sea.
Fisher of soles, did you reflect
the water you walked on
contains so very many souls,
the living and the dead,
you could never begin to count them?

Somewhere a god waits,
rod in hand,
to add you to their number.

Derek Mahon

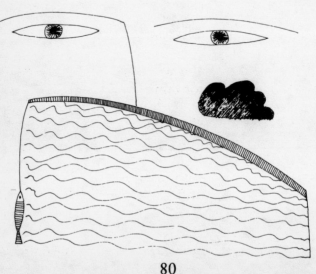

Terminal

She's withering
before our eyes

and no one
noticeably

cries
We do

the hopeful
ritual

each day
we bring

fresh fruit
we prattle

and we pray
for hours

Her room
is heavy

with the scent
of flowers.

Mervyn Morris

Tropical Death

The fat black woman want
a brilliant tropical death
not a cold sojourn
in some North Europe far/forlorn

The fat black woman want
some heat/hibiscus at her feet
blue sea dress
to wrap her neat

The fat black woman want
some bawl
no quiet jerk tear wiping
a polite hearse withdrawal

The fat black woman want
all her dead rights
first night
third night
nine night
all the sleepless droning
red-eyed wake nights

In the heart
of her mother's sweetbreast
In the shade
of the sun leaf's cool bless
In the bloom
of her people's bloodrest
the fat black woman want
a brilliant tropical death yes

Grace Nichols

83

You Never See a Bright Yellow Hearse

The English don't die they just become discreet
You never see a hearse clamped on Harley Street
Or parked at a picnic site
Near Lovers' Leap

You never see a hearse outside a betting shop
Left next to a row of prams
You never see the route to the cemetery
Served by special hearse trams

You never see a hearse at a wedding
Or on adverts for banks
Or a row of hearses at a military parade
Behind a squadron of tanks

Or outside a nightclub at closing time
With racing stripes down the bonnet
Or a hearse at the Motor Show
With dead models draped upon it

You never see a double-decker hearse
Or a hearse that's extra wide
Or a hearse with four or five coffins
All crammed up inside

You never see a coffin in a side car
For a fanatical ex-biker
Or a hearse at a transport cafe
Picking up a hitch-hiker

You never see a hearse used for ram-raiding
Or a hearse with fluffy dice
Or a hearse with a taxi meter
So you can keep an eye on the price

You never see a hearse at an auction
Some dealer's trying to flog
Or a hearse with a trailer
For someone who died with their dog

Each hearse is black and clean and neat
Because the English don't die they just become
    discreet.

Henry Normal

The Lark

The lark from his nest in a hoofprint springs
Up, up and up, trilling dew from his wings,
And busily rests, and sings, and sings.
I watch and listen, wondering why
His song's sad sweetness, a laughing sigh,
Reminds me only that I must die.

Robert Nye

Girl in Tin Photograph

I've been squashed
inside this little leather book
for one hundred years.
If you search for the porch
I'm standing on
you'll find it.
After you're finished
talking about my good dress
and huge hairbow
and have stopped tapping this tin picture
and joking around –
blow the dust off my face,
leave me in peace.

Julie O'Callaghan

87

Stillborn

what we are lamenting
is what has not been
and what will not have seen
this mild May morning

what we are lamenting
is unsuckled air
and what was brought to bear
this mild May morning

what we are lamenting
is the blood and puppy fat, our child,
that has not laughed or cried
this mild May mourning

what we are lamenting
is the life we crave
snatched from the cradle to the grave
this mild May morning

Dennis O'Driscoll

Anthem for Doomed Youth

What passing-bells for these who die as cattle?
Only the monstrous anger of the guns.
Only the stuttering rifles' rapid rattle
Can patter out their hasty orisons.
No mockeries now for them; no prayers nor bells,
Nor any voice of mourning save the choirs, –
The shrill, demented choirs of wailing shells;
And bugles calling for them from sad shires.

What candles may be held to speed them all?
Not in the hands of boys, but in their eyes
Shall shine the holy glimmers of good-byes.
The pallor of girls' brows shall be their pall;
Their flowers the tenderness of patient minds,
And each slow dusk a drawing-down of blinds.

Wilfred Owen

Pipe Dream

If I could choose the hour in which
    Death chooses me,
  And the way in which
It will make its arbitrary choice,
I can think of nothing better than
To fall asleep near midnight in a boat
    As it enters a new port,
      In a boat
With a clarity of stars above
    And below it,
  And all around me
Bright music and voices laughing in
  A language not known to me.
    I'd like to go that way,
      Tired and glad,
With all my future before me,
  Hungry still for the fat
    And visible globe.

Brian Patten

The Tree and the Pool

'I don't want my leaves to drop,' said the tree.
'I don't want to freeze,' said the pool.
'I don't want to smile,' said the sombre man.
'Or ever to cry,' said the Fool.

'I don't want to open,' said the bud.
'I don't want to end,' said the night.
'I don't want to rise,' said the neap-tide.
'Or ever to fall,' said the kite.

They wished and they murmured and whispered,
They said that to change was a crime.
Then a voice from nowhere answered,
'You must do what I say,' said Time.

Brian Patten

Change

Change
Said the sun to the moon,
You cannot stay.

Change
Says moon to the waters,
All is flowing.

Change
Says the field to the grass,
Seed-time and harvest,
Chaff and grain.

You must change,
Said the worm to the bud,
Though not to a rose,

Petals fade
That wings may rise
Borne on the wind.

You are changing,
said death to the maiden, your wan face
To memory, to beauty.

Are you ready to change?
Says thought to the heart, to let pass
All your life long

For the unknown, the unborn
In the alchemy
Of the world's dream?

You will change,
Say the stars to the sun,
Says night to the stars.

Kathleen Raine

Thought at Central Station

Sunday evening. A railway terminus.
Death, you feel, must be
Something like this.

Not, you understand,
Like the end of a journey
Or even its beginning,

But rather the confluence
Of silence and trapped sunlight,
The feeling of a certain aimlessness.

Patrick Ramsey

Beaker Burial

To be sung wistfully, in the style of the late Bud Flanagan

Oh, it's no fun being under
a blooming great megalith
when you've got no one
to be
dead
with.

Death wasn't quite so lonely
when every Ancient Brit
was headed for the good old
communal
cremation
pit.

Then came the Beaker Folk
over the wave;
they said, 'From now on, son,
it's one man
one
grave.'

Curled up like a foetus,
I rot and complain;
just me and my beakers
under
Salisbury
Plain.

Vicki Raymond

Song

When I am dead, my dearest,
Sing no sad songs for me;
Plant thou no roses at my head,
Nor shady cypress tree:
Be the green grass above me
With showers and dewdrops wet;
And if thou wilt, remember,
And if thou wilt, forget.

I shall not see the shadow,
I shall not feel the rain;
I shall not hear the nightingale
Sing on, as if in pain;
And dreaming through the twilight
That doth not rise nor set,
Haply I may remember,
And haply may forget.

Christina Rossetti

When my Grandaddy Died

When my grandaddy died
they weren't sure what to do
with his false teeth and his
one glass eye
and it is this
I sometimes think about
when there's a hot dog left over
at the end of the day
that nobody ate.
My grandaddy's glass eye
would confuse you,
because you weren't sure
which side of his nose
to look to
since
it wasn't real clear
which eye worked and which didn't.
I used to wonder
how he felt
having that marble stuck in his socket
like a stuffed moose.
And did he worry it might
pop out backwards into the gray meat
of his brain?
Or maybe fall into his spaghetti
when he was out with Grandma
at some nice Italian restaurant?

They finally buried
his eye and his teeth
out in the woods
behind the house.
I have thought about that a lot,
and just as I don't like
throwing out
a perfectly good hot dog
at closing time,
I hate to think there's
some other old man
who might could use
a good glass eye
or some teeth
and having to do without
just because Grandmama
didn't want to be
disrespectful.

Cynthia Rylant

Dead Dog

One day I found a lost dog in the street.
The hairs about its grin were spiked with blood,
And it lay still as stone. It must have been
A little dog, for though I only stood
Nine inches for each one of my four years
I picked it up and took it home. My mother
Squealed, and later father spaded out
A bed and tucked my mongrel down in mud.

I can't remember any feeling but
a moderate pity, cool, not swollen-eyed;
Almost a godlike feeling now it seems.
My lump of dog was ordinary as bread.
I have no recollection of the school
Where I was taught my terror of the dead.

Vernon Scannell

The Death King

I hired a carpenter
to build my coffin
and last night I lay in it,
braced by a pillow,
sniffing the wood,
letting the old king
breathe on me,
thinking of my poor murdered body,
murdered by time,
waiting to turn stiff as a field marshal,
letting the silence dishonor me,
remembering that I'll never cough again.

Death will be the end of fear
and the fear of dying,
fear like a dog stuffed in my mouth,
fear like dung stuffed up my nose,
fear where water turns into steel,
fear as my breast flies into the Disposall,
fear as flies tremble in my ear,
fear as the sun ignites in my lap,
fear as night can't be shut off,
and the dawn, my habitual dawn,
is locked up forever.

Fear and a coffin to lie in
like a dead potato.
Even then I will dance in my fire clothes,
a crematory flight,
binding my hair and my fingers,
wounding God with his blue face,
his tyranny, his absolute kingdom,
with my aphrodisiac.

Anne Sexton

The Truth the Dead Know

For my mother, born March 1902, died March 1959
and my father, born February 1900, died June 1959

Gone, I say and walk from the church,
refusing the stiff procession to the grave,
letting the dead ride alone in the hearse.
It is June. I am tired of being brave.

We drive to the Cape. I cultivate
myself where the sun gutters from the sky,
where the sea swings in like an iron gate
and we touch. In another country people die.

My darling, the wind falls in like stones
from the whitehearted water and when we touch
we enter touch entirely. No one's alone.
Men kill for this, or for as much.

And what of the dead? They lie without shoes
in their stone boats. They are more like stone
than the sea would be if it stopped. They refuse
to be blessed, throat, eye and knucklebone.

Anne Sexton

Aye, But to Die

Aye, but to die, and go we know not where;
To lie in cold obstruction and to rot;
This sensible warm motion to become
A kneaded clod; and the delighted spirit
To bathe in fiery floods, or to reside
In thrilling region of thick-ribbed ice;
To be imprison'd in the viewless winds,
And blown with restless violence round about
The pendant world; or be worse than worst
Of those that lawless and incertain thoughts
Imagine howling; 'tis too horrible!
The weariest and most loathed worldly life
That age, ache, penury and imprisonment
Can lay on nature is a paradise
To what we fear of death.

William Shakespeare
Act III, scene i, Measure for Measure

Ozymandias

I met a traveller from an antique land
Who said: Two vast and trunkless legs of stone
Stand in the desert. Near them on the sand,
Half sunk, a shatter'd visage lies, whose frown
And wrinkled lip and sneer of cold command
Tell that its sculptor well those passions read
Which yet survive, stamp'd on these lifeless things,
The hand that mock'd them and the heart that fed;
And on the pedestal these words appear:
'My name is Ozymandias, king of kings:
Look on my works, ye Mighty, and despair!'
Nothing beside remains. Round the decay
Of that colossal wreck, boundless and bare,
The lone and level sands stretch far away.

Percy Bysshe Shelley

Summer Evening

The neighbours play mah-jong.
You can hear their tiles
over the murmur of traffic.
They have been mated so long

their bodies have coalesced
in the lapping candlelight.
Their two masks, neither comic
nor tragic, but neutralized,

enact a phantom history.
They lay out their hands.
The lady's silver hair sparkles
with memories of former glory.

It is too early to go to bed.
Her husband does the reckoning.
Their joint account with death
is finally in the red.

Their game ended, they snuff
the candle and sit quietly.
Now it is only the stars
and the certainty of life.

Norman Silver

Ladybird

This morning in England
because it was sunny
and the doctor agreed
we moved your chair into the garden

A ladybird settled on your faded shawl
and you smiled and said
your house was on fire
though you had no children at home

And the old yellow sun
rocked to sleep
in the striped canvas chair

This afternoon
between coffee and cake
you grew old

You murmured in a strange tongue
called for your mother
and your mother's mother

And the sad yellow sun rocked
alone and forever locked
in the prison stripes of the canvas chair
and the ladybird flew away home.

Valerie Sinason

Petals of Ointment

For my grandmother dying

Nanna closing,
          petals of ointment
so softly
I can hardly hear

But I stop asking her to open

She is returning to herself
in a closing
of indefinable richness

I stroke her cheek
               downwards
the right way

No last ruffling
last rifling from the centre of the core

I have my store of moon-seed
thank you, Nanna

I fold her arms together
old white on white

In her hands
she cradles the newness of her death

like a budding
            moon.

Valerie Sinason

Epitaph for a Gardener

All his life a soldier in the field
at war with the weeds, the grass
rooting back faster than he tore it up.
At peace now it blows over him: *green, green.*

Ken Smith

The Plum's Heart

I've climbed in trees
To eat, and climbed
Down to look about
This world, mouth red
From plums that were
Once clouds in March
– rain I mean, that
Pitiless noise against
Leaves and branches.
Father once lifted me
Into one, and from
A distance I might
Have been a limb,
Moving a little heavier
Than most but a limb
All the same. My hands
Opened like mouths,
The juice running
Without course down
My arms, as I stabbed
For plums, bunched
Or half-hidden behind
Leaves. A bird fluttered
From there, a single
Leaf cutting loose,
And gnats like smoke
Around a bruised plum.

I climbed searching
For those red globes,
And with a sack filled,
I called for father
To catch – father
Who would disappear
Like fruit at the end
Of summer, from a neck
Wound some say – blood
Running like the juice
Of these arms. I
Twisted the throat
Of the sack, tossed
It, and started down
To father, his mouth
Already red and grinning
Like the dead on their
Rack of blackness
When I jumped, he was
Calling, arms open,
The sack at his feet
For us, the half-bitten,
Who bring on the flies.

Gary Soto

The Compromise

He wanted to be buried on the moon.
At last he was answering the question
but she wouldn't have it. She laughed
and he laughed, but he persisted.
He brought it up at dinner parties.
He wrapped it in a joke, but she
knew he meant it. A guest said
there wouldn't be many at the funeral.
No maggots, though, another said,
and no graffiti on the gravestone,
at least for a decade or three.
She brought up the cost. He shrugged,
spoke of sponsorship, of ice-
preservation, of the enabling future.
He would be famous dead. A guest
proposed a grave on Iona, among
the graves of kings. Mentioned
that only twice had men landed
on the moon, and they were living.
Suggested writing to one. And asking
about grave-sites, she added.
He was undeflected. He repeated
he wanted to be buried on the moon,
whatever it took. He went quiet.
A fifth cork was popped, then he
offered a compromise, a heart-coffin
snug in the hold of a space-shuttle,

his heart in there, the rest of him
in Highgate, in Derry, in the sea.
They were all delighted to agree.

Matthew Sweeney

Fishbones Dreaming

Fishbones lay in the smelly bin.
He was a head, a backbone and a tail.
Soon the cats would be in for him.

He didn't like to be this way.
He shut his eyes and dreamed back.

Back to when he was fat, and hot on a plate.
Beside green beans, with lemon juice
squeezed on him. And a man with a knife
and fork raised, about to eat him.

He didn't like to be this way.
He shut his eyes and dreamed back.

Back to when he was frozen in the freezer.
With lamb cutlets and minced beef and prawns.
Three months he was in there.

He didn't like to be this way.
He shut his eyes and dreamed back.

Back to when he was squirming in a net,
with thousands of other fish, on the deck
of a boat. And the rain falling
wasn't wet enough to breathe in.

He didn't like to be this way.
He shut his eyes and dreamed back.

Back to when he was darting through the sea,
past crabs and jellyfish, and others
like himself. Or surfacing to jump for flies
and feel the sun on his face.

He liked to be this way.
He dreamed hard to try and stay there.

Matthew Sweeney

117

How Can You Write a Poem When You're Dying of AIDS?

How can you write a poem when you're dying of
    AIDS,
When you have a reputation for maintaining poetic
    grades?
You write with clarity and elegance
And what you produce might just be flatulence.

The poem is too harsh – too incisive – too intrusive.
How can you write a poem when you're dying of
    AIDS?
I've read the schmaltz – the badly written – the
    desperate,
They cannot squeeze their tears on to the keyboards.

They hide as we all hide.
Being open we hide and being hidden we hide.
How can you write a poem when you're dying of
    AIDS?

I was beautiful.
Now in restaurants people stare at my disfigurements;
They are afraid.
I am afraid.
The good ones don't know what to say,
The bad ones run.

'But James how do you feel about dying?'
HOW THE FUCK DO YOU THINK I FEEL
    ABOUT DYING!
I am 35,
I had a potentially brilliant career ahead of me,
All my ambitions were lying in front of me
Waiting to be picked off like ducks in a gallery,
And I was a good shot.

How can you write a poem when you're dying of
    AIDS?
When the drugs in you fight to get the best side-
    effects.
When the morphine makes you wander unaware and
    incontinent.
When the steroids in reducing your swellings make
    you swell.
When the painkillers give you headaches.

How can you write a poem when you're dying of
    AIDS?
When you crawl to your family – your brother –
    your sister.

I say, 'I know you have to be ashamed of me,
I know your neighbours must never know
For if they did your loving friends might talk about
    you.
So I won't go on telly.
I did go on the radio but only so that you would
    never know.
I won't even appear in my home town in case a
    neighbour sees me.

119

(Though last year, sister, you wanted the neighbour
    to see
the big shiny Volvo I drove).'
I make all these concessions crawling on my knees
    because
I NEED YOUR LOVE.
You spit on me.

How can you write a poem when you're dying of
    AIDS?
Your real friends are helpless and hopeless.
They want to help but I haven't got the strength to
    tell
Them how.
They get depressed.
I get guilty.

How can you write a poem when you're dying of
    AIDS?
MY LOVER ALAN I CANNOT WRITE OF HIM.

How can you write a poem when you're dying of
    AIDS?
When you are such a burden to so many.
When you are such a worry to so many.
When you are such an embarrassment to so many.
When if you were an Englishman you'd take the
    honourable way out.
I'm too scared for that.

How can you write a poem when you're dying of
   AIDS?
I can't ... can you?

James Sykes

121

Do Not Go Gentle into That Good Night

Do not go gentle into that good night,
Old age should burn and rave at close of day;
Rage, rage against the dying of the light.

Though wise men at their end know dark is right,
Because their words had forked no lightning they
Do not go gentle into that good night.

Good men, the last wave by, crying how bright
Their frail deeds might have danced in a green bay
Rage, rage against the dying of the light.

Wild men who caught and sang the sun in flight,
And learn, too late, they grieved it on its way,
Do not go gentle into that good night.

Grave men, near death, who see with blinding sight
Blind eyes could blaze like meteors and be gay,
Rage, rage against the dying of the light.

And you, my father, there on the sad height,
Curse, bless, me now with your fierce tears, I pray.
Do not go gentle into that good night.
Rage, rage against the dying of the light.

Dylan Thomas

'Good Night, Willie Lee, I'll See You in the Morning'

Looking down into my father's
dead face
for the last time
my mother said without
tears, without smiles
without regrets
but with civility
'Good night, Willie Lee, I'll see you
in the morning.'
And it was then I knew that the healing
of all our wounds
is forgiveness
that permits a promise
of our return
at the end.

Alice Walker

Strawberry Picking

One day a man came to us
with a small jar, asking permission
to scatter his mother's ashes
in the light that lay like dust
between the rows of Red Gauntlet.

Then we picked strawberries
as if an old woman knelt with us
on that sun-striped hillside,
watching our fat fruit mount
in punnets, eyeing that most luscious,

pouncing on straw, slugs, bird-pecks
our young hands had passed over,
reading weights over our shoulder,
till the farmer called out, 'Time,'
and we walked to where the wind couldn't blow her.

Susan Wicks

And Then What

Then with their hands they would break bread
wave choke phone thump thread

Then with their tired hands slump
at a table holding their head

Then with glad hands hold other hands
or stroke brief flesh in a kind bed

Then with their hands on the shovel
they would bury their dead.

Carol Ann Duffy

Index of First Lines

130

Acknowledgements

The editor and publishers gratefully acknowledge the following for permission to reproduce copyright poems in this book:

'Come From That Window Child' by John Agard from *Mangoes and Bullets*, published by Pluto Press, 1985, copyright © John Agard, 1985, reprinted by kind permission of John Agard, c/o Caroline Sheldon Literary Agency; 'Memento Mori' by Sabahattin Kudret Aksal, translated by Feyyaz Kayacan Fergar, from *Modern Turkish Poetry* edited by Feyyaz Fergar, published by Rockingham Press, 1992, copyright © Estate of Feyyaz Fergar, 1992, reprinted by permission of the Literary Executor, D. Perman; 'Poem' by Simon Armitage from *Kid*, published by Faber and Faber, 1992, copyright © Simon Armitage, 1992, reprinted by permission of the publisher; 'Funeral Blues' by W. H. Auden from *Collected Poems*, published by Faber and Faber, 1976, 1991, copyright © The Estate of W. H. Auden, 1976, 1991, reprinted by permission of the publisher; 'Charlotte, Her Book' by Elizabeth Barlett from *Strange Territory*, published by Peterloo Poets, 1983, copyright © Elizabeth Barlett, 1983, reprinted by permission of the author; 'Reincarnation' by Sujata Bhatt from *Brunizem*, published by Carcanet, 1988, copyright © Sujata Bhatt, 1988, reprinted by permission of the publisher; 'Kirkyard' by George MacKay Brown from *Poems New and Selected*, published by John Murray (Publishers) Ltd, 1971, copyright © George MacKay Brown, 1971, reprinted by permission of the publisher; 'Cat's-eyes' by Conor Carson from *Mound of the Hostages*, published by Writer's Club Associates, 1990, copyright © Conor Carson, 1990, reprinted by permission of the author; 'Who's That Up There?' by Charles Causley from *All Day Saturday*, published by Macmillan, reprinted by permission of David Higham Associates; 'Yama' by Debjani Chatterjee from *I Was That Woman*, published by Hippopotamus Press, 1989, copyright © Dr Debjani Chatterjee, 1989, reprinted by permission of the author; 'the death of thelma sayles' by Lucille Clifton from *Next: New Poems*, published by BOA editions, 1987, copyright © Lucille Clifton, 1987, reprinted by permission of the publisher; 'imagining bear' by Lucille Clifton from *The Book of Light*, published by Copper Canyon Press, 1993, copyright © Copper Canyon Press, 1993, reprinted by permission of Copper Canyon Press, P.O. Box 271, Port Townsend, WA 98368; 'The Dead' and 'Endangered' by Billy Collins from *Questions About Angels*, published by William Morrow and Company Inc., 1991, copyright © Billy Collins, 1991, reprinted by permission of the publisher; 'Tich Miller' by Wendy Cope from *Making Cocoa for Kingsley Amis*, published by Faber and Faber, 1986, copyright © Wendy Cope, 1986, reprinted by permission of the publisher; 'An Unusual Cat-Poem' by Wendy Cope from *Serious Concerns*, published by Faber and Faber, 1992, copyright © Wendy Cope, 1992, reprinted by permission of the publisher; 'My Grandmother's Love Letters' by Hart Crane from *Complete Poems of Hart Crane*, edited by Marc Simon, by permission of Liverlight Publishing Corporation. Copyright © 1933, 1958, 1966 by Liverlight Publishing Corporation. Copyright © 1986 by Marc Simon; 'Killed in Action' by Juliette de Bairacli-Levy from *The Willow Wreath*, published by Bairacli Books, 1948, copyright © Juliette de Bairacli-Levy, 1948, reprinted by permission of the author; 'Pathetic Magic' by Maura Dooley, copyright © Maura Dooley, 1995, reprinted by permission of the author; 'Tullynoe: Tête-à-Tête in the Priest's Parlour' by Paul Durcan from *Jesus, Break His Fall*, published by Raven Arts Press, Dublin, 1980, copyright © Paul Durcan, 1980, reprinted in *A Snail in His Prime*, published by HarperCollins Publishers, reprinted by permission of HarperCollins Publishers; 'The Baffling Dead' by Irene Earis from *Poetry from Aberystwyth VIII*, published by the University of Wales, Aberystwyth, 1993, copyright © Irene Earis, 1993, reprinted by permission of the author; 'The Old Deaths' by Gavin Ewart from *85 Poems*, published by Hutchinson, 1994, copyright © Gavin Ewart, 1994, reprinted by permission of the publisher; 'The Suicides' by Janet Frame from *The Pocket Mirror*, published by The Women's Press Ltd, 1992, reproduced with permission of Curtis Brown Ltd, London, on behalf of Janet Frame, copyright © 1967, 1992 by Janet Frame; 'Dirge for Unwin' by Philip Gross from *The All Nite Café*, published by Faber and Faber, 1993, copyright © Philip Gross, 1993, reprinted by permission of the publisher; 'A Dog Was Crying Tonight In Wicklow Also' by Seamus Heaney, copyright © Seamus Heaney, 1995, reprinted by permission of the author; 'Mid-term Break' by Seamus Heaney from *Death of a Naturalist*, published by Faber and Faber, 1966, 1991, copyright © Seamus Heaney, 1966, 1991, reprinted by permission of the publisher; 'Local Story' by Libby Houston first published as 'Old & Very Much Avoided' in *A Stained Glass Raree Show* by Allison and Busby Ltd, 1967, this version in *Necessity*, published by Slow Dancer Press, 1988, copyright © Libby Houston, 1967, reprinted by permission of the author; 'Every Dying Man' by Jaan Kaplinski from *The Same Sea in Us All*, published by Collins Harvill, 1985, copyright © Jaan Kaplinski and Sam Hamill, 1985, reprinted by permission of the publisher, 'Brendan Gallacher' by Jackie Kay from *Two's Company*, published by Blackie Books, 1992, copyright © Jackie Kay, 1992, reprinted by permission of the author; 'The Stincher' by Jackie Kay from *Three Has Gone*, published by Blackie Books, 1994, copyright © Jackie Kay, 1994, reprinted by permission of the author; 'Grandfather' by Lotte Kramer from *Family Arrivals*, published by Poet & Pringer 1981, copyright © Lotte Kramer, 1981, and 'Post Mortem' from *Desecration of Trees*, published by Hippopotamus Press, 1994, copyright © Lotte Kramer, 1994, reprinted by permission of the author; 'Detour' by Michael Longley from *Gorse Fires*, published by Secker and Warburg, 1991, copyright © Michael Longley, 1991, reprinted by permission of the publisher; 'The Lesson' by Edward Lucie-Smith

133